SILENT ECHOES

A specially crafted collection of
Flash Fiction and Short Stories

D. T. Moorhouse

Also Available By D. T. Moorhouse

Empty Colours Trilogy
Book 1: Purple Shadows

*For my late grandfather, Pat
A true gentleman, never forgotten*

CONTENTS

1. FLASH FICTION

D. T. MOORHOUSE

HER TROUBLED MIND'S REFLECTION

A young girl stumbles through the streets of Paris. Alone. Barefoot. Her dress torn. Blood smeared across her cheek. It's only when you look to your left that you see her. She stares back at you and you turn your head away. But not for long. Something draws your gaze back to her. Something inside forces you to examine her blood-smeared visage. She looks afraid. And, like someone you once knew. From somewhere, or rather some time. But you can't put your finger on it.

You step closer to her until you're only a metre apart. She doesn't say anything. Neither do you. But there's something there between you. A connection. Familiarity you might call it. You want to reach out and help but you can't. Something is holding you back. You hear a voice suddenly beside you. Soft. Tentative. It's a man. He's speaking to you. Asking questions.

"Excuse me, Madam, are you okay?"

You don't answer, your eyes now searching the girl's bemused expression.

"Madam? Madam? Are you in trouble? Have you been attacked? Should I call for help?"

You wonder why he's directing these questions at you. You're not the one in trouble. You tell him this. That it's not you. It's her. But he looks confused. Scared almost.

"Madam I think we should get you some help."

But you don't need help. You tell him this. Again. That it's her. You point to her. But he looks more confused than before. "She needs help," you tell him. "Look at her," you say. "Help her."

"But that is you, Madam," he says, now pointing like you did, to the girl standing in front of you, her arm stretched out in front of her, pointing in your direction. "That's a shop window, Madam. That is your reflection."

****First Published as a Highly Commended
entry in Fish Anthology 2018****

A LETTER FROM HIS FAERIE GIRL

The envelope sat on his bed, just atop the covers, the edges worn, water-stained in spots. Evidence of its recent travels, perhaps. And innocuous though it seemed, like any other letter he had received on the outside, this one irked him something fierce. It gnawed away at him, irritated him, made him feel uncomfortable in a way he couldn't explain. Whenever he tried to pick it up it was as though his fine motor skills stuttered to a halt and he was left grasping at empty air above the bed. If he even so much as dared to look at the envelope it was as though something grabbed his insides and twisted.

But it was just paper. And ink. To an outsider, there could have been nothing about this small, white envelope that was making his life more miserable than it already was. It did not possess the ability to hurt him, not more than he had already been hurt anyway. Yet, somehow, it did.

Still, amidst all of the hurt, he longed to open it, to devour its contents, to see her words, written in the same sloping script that she had written his name with on the outside.

He longed to be able to imagine her in the act of writing, choosing her words carefully, under a tree outside perhaps, under the heavens. His faerie girl. Pouring words, chosen just for him and only him, onto paper.

He hated how much the thought of her made him smile. Because smiling meant happiness. And he didn't understand happiness. Maybe once, long ago he did. Not now though, after so long. Anger was better. Anger was easier. Anger, he understood. Anger understood him.

And so all he had to do, for the smile to vanish and for anger to bubble serenely within, was to think, that though the words she had chosen were just for him, his would not be the only eyes to fall upon them. There would always be a middle man, an overseer of their relationship. Reading her words, perhaps mocking, never savouring them, lovingly, as he did.

He had lied and told her once, how the letters, were, in a way, like them almost touching. But her touch would always be marred and tainted, corrupted by the middleman, as he scanned her writing, searching, for a code, a keyword, something... to deny him her innermost thoughts.

And though it hurt, though his discomfort was now at its peak and though anger was so firmly nestled within him, he still longed to tear it open, to pull the pages from the already violated envelope, to unfold that first page and inhale the faint traces of her musky perfume. Though that may have just been his imagination...

It was so close, there, on that thin mattress. So he reached out, rested his fingers on the innocent white rectangle, admiring that sloped handwriting, how she wrote his name with such delicacy. And the number after it, which he actively tried to ignore...

He slid his finger along the seal, but he heard them then, the other inmates, starting to move about, becoming restless in their confinement, his cellmate starting to wash his hands in their tiny shared sink, getting ready for their allocated time in the courtyard.

He decided, as the buzzer sounded somewhere above and the locks clicked open, that he would read it later, his calloused fingers placing that seemingly innocuous envelope under his sorry excuse for a pillow, beside the others.

He had, after all, got time.

COLD RUSSIAN SUMMER

I was born, in Moscow, to a Russian oligarch and his part-time lover in the summer of 1987. It was colder than usual for that time of year, my mother used to tell me. My father said he did not care what the fucking temperature was, that he did not care that the azaleas in the garden were not in bloom and that he did not care how many blankets my mother had wrapped around her or how many pillows she had to have propped up behind her back as she screamed and strained until I popped out, screaming, crying and covered in amniotic crap, into one of the waiting nurse's arms.

He often told me that he did not care. About me. About my mother. About anything other than the money that passed through his calloused, blood-stained hands. But my mother cared. She cared more than anyone. Cared about *me* more than anyone. And I will never forget how much she cared, how much she showed her love for me and how, even on my birthday, as my father splattered her brains all over the walls of his study, she tried to protect me, yelling for me to run, to hide, to escape before he turned to me.

But I did not run. I could not. I stayed and watched, as he hit her again and again, the golf club in his hands flicking pieces of her around the room as he raised it each time before landing another squelching strike. I watched until her head was but a mush of bloody grey matter, scattered across every available surface in that study.

It was only after he had put the titanium golf club down and used the back of his hand to wipe away the foam that had gathered at the corners of his mouth that he turned to me, the young girl in her silk nightdress, standing still beside the blazing fireplace. I think he expected me to run, I am not sure. I still cannot say definitively what expression lay on his face at that moment.

But what I can conclude, without a shadow of a doubt, is that it did not remain on his face for long, nor did the poker he used regularly to tend to the fire stay in my hand for long. It found itself poking his charred, wreck of a heart. Because it was his turn. To suffer. To feel just a fraction of the pain that he had inflicted upon me and my mother since that unusually cold summer of 1987.

And it was my turn to tell him, as I stood watching blood pour out of his chest, that *I* did not care.

FUN FILLED FIELDS OF SORROW

An open field. Tulips and dandelions. Some mature, others just barely blooming. The wind blowing. Wafting effortlessly. They sway in unison. Gently. A trampled path snakes through the flowers. The path ends at a deadened circle. Centered is a woman. She spins and sings, spins and sings. Smiling. Her dress is billowing. Catching wind. Rising and falling. Dancing to the sound of her voice. The children surround her. Giggling, cheering. Happiness abounds. They join hands. Run in circles. The woman spins right. The children run left. The wind gets stuck between them. Creating a vortex. Travelling. Faster and faster. Building and building. The giggling grows louder. The singing grows stronger. A crescendo will come crashing. Suddenly a bang. Another. One child falls. A second. Third. Fourth. All fall. The woman stops, her spinning ceased. Her song now silent. But, her smile remains. She counts the dead. Lowers her gun. Her aim was pure.

Not one remains. She beckons and the men come in. They lift the dead imposters. Their heads loll, the blood seeps down. Arms covered. Hair matting. They follow the path back, the woman behind, rifle upon her shoulder. A solemn march. Though still, she smiles. They reach the church. The people watch. Eyes wide. Holding their heads high. The priests await. Bibles clasped in shaky grips. They move aside and the bodies are dropped. One atop the other. The bearers approach, torches gripped tight. They touch them to the heads and clothes. The flames grow high as the priests chant. The men step back. Hold their wives in bloodstained arms. A sigh sweeps through the watching crowd. They stay until the flesh has gone. Charred bones upon the altar. The gun-wielding woman is the first to leave. The others follow swiftly. They see her out quickly. Out of town. Out of life. Their troubles now forgotten. But not hers. Never hers. She heads to the next one. Walking fast. Reloading. Preparing. Smiling. Another field awaits.

A WARM HEARTH IN ABEYANCE

I lifted the chipped cup to my lips, stopped before the steaming liquid entered my mouth and frowned, my eyebrows meeting over the bridge of my nose, the skin on my forehead crinkling. Something wasn't right. I could feel a chill in the air, my skin tingling, goosebumps threatening to make their way to the surface of my arms.

Placing the cup on the countertop beside the ancient copper kettle, I turned and made my way out into the narrow hallway. My steps echoed on the cracked tiles, the clip-clop sound of heels on ceramic bouncing off the bare walls, coming back and settling somewhere inside my ears.

I reached the door, yanked it open and felt around in the dark with one hand, my other gripping the door frame tightly so I wouldn't lose my balance. My hand came to rest on the surface of the hot water tank. Freezing.

I retracted my hand, suppressing an angry, resentful sigh, cursing the day I took this old manor off the market. Still, I made a mental note to call a plumber, adding it to the ever-growing list of things that needed fixing, the ever-growing list of major renovations needed, knowing that it would be months before I could pull together enough funds, even to afford the call out charge.

I should have sold the fucking thing.

THROUGH A BROKEN LENS

Young Francie Hogan stumbled through the farmer's market. He stopped beside the rancid, foul-smelling cattle pens, where the wet-nosed Shorthorns breathed and mooed heavily, their breath rising in clouds of steam on the cold morning air. The farmer's son clawed gently at his chest, having just noticed the missing weight of his new Canon camera from around his neck.

"Oh! My camera!"

Francie swore loudly, startling the cows nearest to him. They scrambled towards the opposite corner of their cramped pen and he turned, trudging through the mud, making his way back to where his father had parked the Land Rover, in the hopes that he had left it there, his green shin-high wellington boots squelching with each step.

"Don't wander too far now Francie, it's nearly time for your tea." The voice belonged to a tall, grey-haired man, following behind, his long brown overcoat zipped up tightly to guard against the crisp morning air.

"I'm looking for my camera!" Francie's tone was somewhat defensive as he surveyed the man. He did not recognise him.

"Oh, why didn't you say Francie! The big Canon isn't it?" The man seemed to think for a moment, glancing back at the market stalls they had passed a moment ago. "I think I might have spotted it over at Mr. Brennan's stall on my travels."

"Did you really?" There was a hint of desperation in Francie's voice now, a slight frustration bubbling within him, as his father had already scolded him, rather too harshly earlier in the week, for allowing a large number of prized sheep to escape from their enclosure. They had caused chaos on the main road. Losing his expensive new camera would not be well received.

"Yes, I'm sure of it, now that I think about it. Why don't you have a look, Francie." The tall man grinned and watched as the young man made his way back through the slippery mud.

Old Mr. Brennan was, of course, the sort that would pick up an expensive camera, without bothering to find out who it belonged to, Francie thought to himself as he approached the elderly man known for his wheeling and dealing antics, sitting in his stained travel chair.

"Ah, Francie, m'boy, how's the form today? Isn't it your father who usually handles the purchases? Is he coming along?"

"I don't know, I'm not here to buy, I was just looking for my camera, actually." Francie spoke indignantly, not sure if he was going to have to prove his ownership over it before he could get it back. Though how he could do that now he didn't know...

"A camera?" Mr. Brennan's, bushy eyebrows contracted, meeting over his hairy, bulbous nose. "I haven't seen any cameras Francie. Maybe over by O'Reilly. They're more his sort of thing." He struggled out of his chair and sauntered over to one of the farmers who had stopped nearby, examining the merchandise on offer.

So once again, Francie trudged through the mounds of mud, his desperation growing, beads of sweat gathering at his temples, threatening to roll down his face if he didn't wipe them soon. His father had never approved of his hobby and losing his Canon, which he had forked out hundreds for, would only give him further reason to chastise his only son. He needed to find it. That camera was his only escape from the monotonous, panopticon that was the family farm.

"Mrs. Clancy, Mrs. Clancy! Francie was practically shouting now as he tried to jog towards a small, stout woman, whose face had been prematurely aged by the weather, deep lines etched into her sallow skin.

"Ah Francie, how are ya?" She smiled warmly at him, the lines by her eyes creasing even further as her cheeks forced the skin upwards.

"Not too good, Mrs. Clancy. I've lost my camera." Francie was breathless now. "Have you seen it?"

"I haven't I'm afraid, Francie, dear. Did you look by O' Reilly's stall? They're more his sort of thing..."

"And he does this every day?" A slender woman in a white

coat, with a small visitors badge clipped to the left lapel, turned to the tall, grey-haired man who had been observing Francie all morning.

"Indeed he does. It appears that his psychosis has manifested itself in a form of hallucinated purgatory, forcing him to constantly relive the day before his breakdown, over and over." He smiled thinly and rubbed his hands together, already anticipating the next question from the visiting clinician.

"Have you considered just giving the patient his camera? Seeing how he reacts, if the situation changes?"

"Of course, we have, and we would… if we had access to it."

"I don't understand." The woman followed the man from the high dependency ward, in which Francie was now speaking pointedly at the bedside cabinet, pulling at his hair with both hands and cursing loudly.

"Well, you see, it's in evidence at Knocknaree Garda Station. He used it to cave his father's skull in."

HIS FAVOURITE PLACE IN THE UNIVERSE

I stand over the empty grave and remember the words my father said to me as we stood at this very spot almost twenty years previously, his eyes closed, arms spread wide, head pointed to the sky.

"Remember this place, Lena. Remember it. Absorb it. Take in every detail. Remember how the soil crunches under your feet. Remember the many beautiful colours of the leaves on the trees that surround us, Lena. Listen to how they rustle with each passing of the wind. Listen to how the wind whispers to you from behind them, how it calls to you, tells you the most wonderful stories. Remember this place, Lena. This is my favourite place in the entire universe."

As I turn and walk to the rear of my car parked several meters away I wish that I was remembering my father's words fondly. Because at the time, as I stood in that copse with my father, I was truly in awe. My father, a man who had never expressed any emotion, at least not publicly, was sharing with me his love for this place of wonder and beauty. And for close to twenty years that memory lay nestled in my heart, untarnished. A perfect moment in my life.

Until I discovered the truth. About him. About what he had done. About all of the innocent people he had destroyed.

Now, as I drag his body from the trunk across the earth, I think of the anger that bubbled within me as he admitted what he had done. It was as though my whole body had been taken over and I had surrendered all control to some being borne of anger and destruction. Then, before I knew it, the statuette that sat on his mantle, of a violinist in her white flowing dress, was cracking his skull open onto the hardwood floor of his living room, the blood oozing out, creating a perfect pool of deepest crimson.

Now, as I pat down the last of the soil and grip the shovel tight with both hands, I feel warm tears begin to trickle down my cheeks. But I am not crying for my father. I will never again shed a tear for that bastard. No, I am weeping now for a memory destroyed, a memory that needs to be forgotten. A perfect memory of beauty and wonder, that must now be left behind. With him. Here. In his favourite place in the universe.

TOGETHER

T he whitewashed fence glistened under the glaring heat of the mid-July sun. Mr. Evans stood on his porch, gazing out at the glorious day before him, one hand resting on the wooden beam to his right, his other holding onto the wireless house phone tightly, waiting.

He watched as the sprinkler across the way in Mrs. Hackett's lawn flared into life, slowly tch, tch, tch-ing backwards and forwards, giving the parched, neatly clipped grass its much-needed draught of life. The old man, with his top two shirt buttons undone and plimsoles hastily stuffed onto the wrong feet, noted the two BMX bicycles that lay abandoned two houses down outside the Robinson household, laying on their sides on the footpath, handlebars askew.

He smiled to himself, remembering days of old when he would ride with Lola to the creek. He recalled, fondly, how they too would leave their two-speed bicycles to sizzle under the heat of the summer sun as they ran delightedly to the water. On the way he would grab Lola by the waist and spin her around, disorienting her so he could get there first, relishing the thought of splashing about in the water. But he would never go in first. Never. He would hover by the water's edge, his heart beating, his fingertips full of electricity, until Lola had caught up to him, laughing, smiling and slipped her hand into his. He would grab it tightly, bring his lips to meet hers and they would wade in, together.

As he watched down the street, the high pitched wailing grew louder and he saw the large vehicle careen around the corner, the inner wheels scraping off the edge of the footpath. The two men sitting in the front seats craned their necks from side to side, looking up the beautifully manicured lawns in turn, to the shiny brass plates attached to the walls beside the doors, searching for the correct house number.

As it approached, Mr. Evans stood a little straighter and stretched his hand slowly in their direction to let them know they had reached the right place. The tyres ground to a stop, crunching on the asphalt and the two men alighted, frantic and determined. One of them went straight to the back of the vehicle and swung the two doors open with force, while the other raced up the lawn to Mr. Evans, looking sombre but professional.

The old man couldn't register what was being said to him by the paramedic so he just pointed through the open door, into the house, his head nodding solemnly, his words just barely audible as he uttered them. "Just through there, on the right. You needn't rush though, she's already gone."

Now as he stands just inside the narrow hallway, the phone back in its cradle on the side table, the house empty of all but himself, he looks at the sun streaming in through the window of the dining room, its rays falling upon the dark oak wood of the table. He lets out a gentle sob and wipes away a single tear as he remembers fondly the days of old when he and Lola would exit the water and flop down onto the grass beside their bikes, their hands entwined, waiting, for that beaming mid-July sun to dry them out so they could head back home. Together.

YOU DO NOT SWIM IN LOCKLEAR LAKE

You didn't swim in Locklear Lake. You just didn't. Everyone knew it. The frail old lady who came with a bag of bread for the ducks every day knew it. The little kid, with his motorised toy boat that was left there because it went out of range and he couldn't wade in to get it back, knew it. Even the tourists, with their fanny packs full of holiday essentials such as a pocket-sized sun lotion or a crudely folded map of the area, knew that you didn't dip even a single toe into the bright red water of Locklear Lake.

But I didn't know it. Not then anyway.

When the news of what happened spread, most people said I was naive, that I was stupid, that someone my age should have known better. But I wasn't those things. I was just oblivious. I hadn't heard the warnings. I couldn't see that the water glowed a deep crimson. To me, it seemed like any other lake. Empty, apart from the strange-looking ducks, sure, but calm, even pleasant looking. Perfect to cool off in after a long cycle through a new town. At least that was until I felt the fire penetrate my very soul. Until the flesh started to peel away from my bones. Until I scrambled back onto the shore, the sinew and tendons on my arms and legs exposed. Until the earth-shattering screams that escaped from my throat alerted those nearest.

But now I know.

And now, when I see the frail old lady bend a little too close to throw the remnants of her bread to the ducks or see a little kid inch closer to keep his boat in close range, I shout out a warning. I shout for them to stay back, to keep away from the flames. But they don't hear. They never hear. They just turn and walk away, sparing the swiftest of glances for the small brass plaque, a memorial, dedicated to the girl that should have listened to the warnings, the girl who should not have been so stupid.

Because, as everybody around here knows: You Do Not Swim in Locklear Lake.

SWEET TREACLE TARTS

I hold my breath as the cold gel comes into contact with my skin. The bump is barely noticeable, looking almost as if I have been simply overindulging on sweet treacle tarts in the evenings. But it isn't just the remnants of a sickly sweet pudding inside me. No. It is more. Much more. I can feel it. It is something new. Something strange. Something very much alive within me, changing the very fabric of my being.

I close my eyes as the hard plastic is pressed against my gel-covered flesh and a light pressure is applied. I feel it pass back and forth, the search now well and truly underway. I haven't told Simon yet. In fact, I haven't told anyone bar the pretty blonde girl at reception who noted my details in their system and now the rather masculine looking nurse who looks for signs of life, waiting for the unmistakable soft whooshing noise of a heartbeat.

I raise my head as the search continues, the strokes becoming more frantic, the pressure on my soft flesh increasing. I see the nurse's brow furrow, her eyebrows coming together just above the bridge of her nose. She presses a series of buttons on the monitor, pushing harder still on my stomach, the sensation now becoming one of discomfort. She drops her hand, replaces the probe to its holster and wipes my stomach clean with a wet wipe. I watch as her expression falters, changes, then settles, a sadness now evident in her eyes that was absent a moment ago.

I shake my head gently as the nurse takes my hand into hers and tells me what I already know, have already realised. There is no change. There will be no soft whooshing noise gracing my ears. There are absolutely no signs of life at all.

Perhaps it was just sweet treacle tarts after all.

THE WHISPERS

The whispers came on my eighth birthday.

There was no party. No pointy hats or gift bags. No ice cream, cake, or clowns. Mom couldn't afford it. Any of it. She couldn't afford much of anything. And I resented her for that. Deeply. Blamed her for what I became, for everything I did. But I realise now that it wasn't her fault. None of it. It never was. Not even what happened after.

They stopped when I turned twelve.

Too late. I had already become something different. Something that scared the other kids. Something that crept into their brains and unsettled them. They ran. Which was good. Because it wasn't a nice time for the people that got too close to me. Anyone that was there at the time will tell you that. If they could. Mom, Gramps, even the doctors. Sure, they tried to help but ultimately they failed, picked off one by one as the whispers consumed me.

They returned when I reached adulthood.

I had forgotten how much they hurt. But they sent me a reminder before too long. And the blood. God, the blood. Everywhere. I was trapped then. Forced into a prison from which they will never let me escape. But not by the whispers. No. They would let me roam, give me freedom. No, it's the others that keep me locked up. They say it's to help me, but really it's to protect themselves.

They have stayed with me since then.

They haven't come and gone like they did before. No, they've been lingering for a while now, controlling me, causing endless amounts of fear for the people around me. Not that there are very many of those left. One a day, and never the same one two days in a row. Never. They learned to rotate. Better for them. Better for me. Because.... the whispers.... the whispers know when someone gets too close. And they will make me kill.

The whispers will never leave.

WHEN ONLY LOVE REMAINS

The dipping sun casts a shadow onto the white-washed beams of the coastal cottage. On the porch a rocking chair sways gently back and forth in the breeze, watching as the waves sweep onto the beach, clearing away the footsteps of the long-married couple just entering the house through the screen door. He carries his shoes by his side, the laces still tied, while she carries their large checkered blanket, draped over her arm, grains of sand dropping from it onto the floor as they make their way to the only bedroom. Once inside, the man places his shoes at the foot of the bed while she sits on the edge, shoulders hunched, head bowed, the blanket resting on her lap.

"I'm so sorry love, I wanted it to be special. Like when we were young." The man's voice is shallow, the words barely passing his lips.

The woman turns and looks at him, a smile tautening the wrinkles on her face. "It's fine, John, really. I still love you."

She reaches out and takes his liver-spotted hand into hers and while she beams, his face remains stoic.

The sun, now almost set, pours in through the window, casting shadows around the room. The old woman, seeing only his silhouette, squints up at her husband's face. She looks for a sign that he is okay but he pulls his hand from hers. He bends and retrieves his shoes from the floor. His hands tremble as he struggles to undo the laces. The woman watches as he slips one foot on, then the other and shuffles across the room.

"John, where are you going? Come sit with me."

He inclines his head toward her, already pulling the door closed behind him.

"I'm sorry love, I wanted it to be special. I really did..."

A SWEET EMBRACE

I kissed her neck, my lips lingering on her soft flesh, the taste sweet as sugar. She brought one hand up and ran it through my hair, the tips of her nimble fingers gliding gently along the surface of my scalp, parting my chestnut coloured curls, sending shivers trickling down my spine. The other she brought down, passing momentarily over my breasts, gently caressing my navel and pushing her finger inside me, followed swiftly by another, a soft moan of pleasure escaping from me with each penetration.

It felt wonderful embracing her like this, feeling the warmth emanating from her, our bodies entangling, merging, becoming one.

But as much as I longed for it to last, for her to be mine forever, it wouldn't. It couldn't. She wasn't ready. To go public. To leave her world and enter mine. But I would wait. I would have to. I loved her too much not to.

THOSE WHO FORGET

An old man, wearing a finely tailored pin-striped suit, climbed the stone steps that rose to meet the mahogany front door of the imposing building in front of him. With each arduous step he took, bones cracked, muscles spasmed, pain struck, contorting the aged man's pallid features into a pained grimace. When he reached the top, he breathed in, his chest expanding as his lungs filled with the air he so desperately needed. He stood on the porch for a moment and took one last look at the letter in his hand, scanning over the address, written in a vaguely familiar script, before folding it over and placing it into his breast pocket. Inside the pocket already his full-grain leather wallet lay nestled against the rich cotton interior.

With one hand resting on the head of his polished, Blackthorn cane, that had once been used more for appearance and status than for actual necessity, the old man leaned forward and raised the other, prepared to ring the doorbell that was set into the wall just beside the large door. But something inside the weary, old body stopped him. Something rose from the pit of his stomach. It reached up and wrapped itself tightly around his chest. His breathing became erratic, his cane wobbled unsteadily on the ground and his outstretched, liver-spotted hand curled into a fist and fell limply back into place at the side of his body.

He couldn't do it.

With a grim sigh through gritted teeth, as pain struck again, Maurice turned away from the door in resignation. He made his way back down the steps with great difficulty, his knees reluctant to bend in the direction needed. The end of his thin, wooden cane made a dull clunk each time it came into contact with the concrete underneath it as he walked away from the building. Clunk, step. Clunk, step. Clunk, step.

He walked along the bustling streets for as long as he could but tiredness was beginning to overcome him and the pain was becoming worse. He needed to sit for a while, rest, wait for the pain to subside, wait for the next burst of energy to come so that he could continue. Then he could go home. And so the finely dressed old man found himself wandering into a busy park, where the hot summer sun was beaming down. Where the smell of freshly mown grass and flowers in full bloom filled the air. Where children played, parents chatted and birds soared freely overhead.

As he walked along the footpath that snaked its way through the neatly mown grass verges, Maurice stumbled upon a rickety old bench. He lowered himself slowly onto it, his cane bending slightly in the middle as his weight pressed down upon it until his bottom came to rest on the weather-beaten wood. As he watched the people around him having fun, enjoying their day, the pain within him subsided. It didn't disappear completely. It never would. It was part of him now. And as the laughter of children filled the air around him, Maurice's eyes grew heavier, until his lids shut completely and his grip on the cane slackened. It fell free of his grip and the short-haired woman, who had been watching him since he entered the park, smiled to herself, rose from her seated position close to the rhodo-dendron bushes and walked away, triumphant.

He woke with a start sometime later, his eyes snapping open, adjusting to the semi-darkness, unsure of where he was or how he had gotten there. He reached into the inside pocket of his suit jacket, to extract his wallet but felt something in there alongside it. He pulled out the piece of folded up paper, unfamiliar to him.

Unfolding it, he found, upon reading the formal greeting, that it was a letter addressed to him. But he shook his head, perplexed, unable to recall receiving a letter. Nor did he remember placing it into the pocket which normally contained just his wallet. Nevertheless, he felt there was a vague familiarity to the slanted script, so he read through it, finding that it instructed him, very clearly and precisely, where to go and who to ask for.

So, believing that it must hold some importance, Maurice rose unsteadily from the bench and began to make his way to the address contained in the letter. Eventually, he came to the correct building and began to climb the stone steps which led to a mahogany front door. He struggled up them, his bones cracking, his muscles spasming, pain striking.

He leaned on the head of his cane with one hand, breathing deeply until his lungs reached their limit of expansion and raised the other to ring the doorbell. But something halted him, prohibiting his hand from travelling any further towards the small white button. Something rose from within the rickety old man, wrapping itself tightly around his chest. His hand hovered in mid-air for a moment, curled into a fist and fell back heavily to his side, confusion and resignation rampant.

He turned away from the door, pain flaring within him and made his way back down the stone steps, the end of his dark coloured cane making a dull clunk each time it came into contact with the concrete underneath it. Clunk, step. Clunk, step. Clunk step.

RELEASE

I feel the chill in the air as I step outside, the thin woollen jumper hanging off my sullen frame, offering minimal protection. The door closes behind me with a soft clang, the latch clicking firmly into place, shutting me out completely.

I don't want to leave. But I have to. My time is up, according to them. I have completed the required hours set out at the hearing last August.

I truly grew to love my time here, how it felt to be clean, to be sober, to be free from the burden that is life. But now I have been thrust back into the wild. With nowhere to go. No-one to go to. No purpose in my heart. No reason to stay clean. But I walk on anyway, glancing at the cars passing alongside me, wondering what it would feel like to stop, turn and step out into their path, to feel, truly, a sense of release.

Time to find out.

SLIPPING AWAY

I tipped the sugar from the spoon into the steaming liquid. I waited for a moment as it settled and dissolved then swirled it around, creating a vortex, the spoon hitting the sides of the worn mug. Clink, swirl. Clink, swirl. Clink, swirl.

I placed the spoon on the counter, a shallow pool of milky tea nestled in its concaved surface and took the mug into my hands, holding it tightly, feeling the warmth emanating from it, spreading through my palms, to my fingers. I stood like this for a moment, savouring the sensation.

Out in the hallway, I climbed, taking the stairs two at a time, eager to get back to him. Inside the room, I settled into the armchair I had brought up from the lounge downstairs when he came home from the hospital. I raised the mug to my lips and blew softly on the hot tea, watching over the rim of the mug as his chest rose and fell gently. Though his eyes remained closed, his consciousness elsewhere. Slowly, peacefully slipping away from the world of the living.

LETTER OF FUTILITY

To my Dearest, Darling Kate,

I had hoped I would never have to write a letter like this, but I am left with no other choice. Our unit falls weaker by the day, our numbers plummeting. The men around me are perishing at alarming rates and our enemies advance upon us at a steady pace, causing untold amounts of destruction and devastation as they progress. It will not be long before they are upon us.

I cannot bear to still be here when they arrive. I have witnessed the brutality they have imposed upon my comrades. I have seen the men, whom I have come to call my brothers over these last sixteen months, suffer the most painful deaths that even the bravest of us could not withstand. I have lost all hope. So it is with regret that I have decided to end it before they come for me.

But please do not think of me as a coward, for I have fought bravely until now. I have tried my hardest to eliminate as many of them as I can but, with each one we destroy, another ten seem to materialise in their place. Our resistance is falling. Not just here but on every battlefield across the world. Our fight is now futile. I cannot envision any outcome in which we survive this brutal invasion. I know it is not what you want to hear but soon these monstrous entities will overtake us all.

We number just twelve men in the compound now and I sense I am not the only one to have made the difficult decision to end it before they come for us. By the time you receive this letter I will have done it. That is if they have not killed me before I have built up the courage. But please do not cry for me. I am saving myself from the pain these monsters would be sure to inflict upon me. I am ending things on my terms.

Stay strong during all that will come. Live the rest of your life while you can. And believe that we will meet again in some form. We are destined to.

Yours Forever and Always,
Dominic x

2. SHORT STORIES

WHAT ARE FRIENDS FOR?

"Go on then, do it." Elsie Hartigan giggled, clasping a hand over her mouth to prevent herself from bursting into a frenzied fit of laughter.

"No way, you do it." Her sister, Macy, dressed in a matching periwinkle blue dress, looked at her, her eyes wide, her mouth threatening to turn into a wide grin, the laughter held reluctantly in her throat.

"One of you just fucking do it, it's not gonna stay hard forever." Jonathan lifted his head, raising it away from the firm, springy mattress to look at the two sisters, his small, erect penis starting to slacken as he waited impatiently for one of them to touch it. Like they had done to Billy Jones.

It was the first time Jonathan's had ever been exposed to anyone that didn't have one of their own to play with and the excitement of it had immediately made it stand to attention, the anticipation bubbling away merrily within him.

But now it had been ten minutes and it was starting to

soften, resting against his hairless inner thigh, instead of pointing up towards the ceiling the way he liked it. His patience, too, was starting to wane. If one of them didn't grip it soon, it would go floppy completely, receding back into the little tuft of scraggly black pubic hair that had seemed to appear out of nowhere six months ago.

"Fine then." Elsie reached her hand out, moving it towards the little pecker but it gave a quick jolt as the blood continued to drain out of it and Elsie pulled her hand back, as if afraid she was about to receive an electric shock. She looked at her sister and the two broke into manic laughter, their high pitched giggles reverberating around the small room, annoying the adolescent boy that lay atop the floral patterned duvet.

"Je-sus Christ." Jonathan stood up quickly and his now almost flaccid penis flopped against the waistband of his trousers. He pulled them up fully, tucked his still untouched member into his underwear and stormed out of the room, doing up his flies as he went, still hearing the two girls' laughter penetrate his thoughts as he walked.

Outside, his friend Louis waited, holding onto the handlebars of both of their BMX bikes, eager to hear all the juicy details of his first handjob from two, real-life girls. But Jonathan just shook his head when he drew level with his best mate and slung his leg over the frame of the bike.

He settled onto the seat, his two arms resting on the black rubber handlebars as he leaned forward, dejected, while his two feet were flat on the ground either side of the front wheel.

"Fucking frigid bitches."

Louis' smile disappeared. "They didn't do it then?"

"No. They didn't even touch it."

"But Billy Jones said-"

"Well, Billy Jones is a fucking liar. Should've known he didn't get a handy off the Hartigan sisters. As if anyone would touch his little bean sprout. Come on." Jonathan kicked off from the ground, pedalling fast, his friend falling in behind him, both of their thoughts on Billy Jones and his story that they now knew was bullshit.

"So, they really didn't do it..." Louis said, when they had cycled along the creek, and stopped under the bridge where they had set up their makeshift den, the wooden pallets they had found a few weeks earlier acting as walls, a raggedy old sheet draped across a gap between two pallets masquerading as a door.

"No, I'd fucking tell you if they did."

"Well, what happened anyway?" Louis held the sheet up for his friend, feeling blood already starting to rush below his waist, just as it always did when they were alone in the den or talking about anything remotely sexual.

"Well, I went in like Billy said and knocked on the door. The skinny one answered. I told her I wanted what Billy got. So she brought me into the bedroom. The other one was already in there, brushing her hair. I sat down on the bed and pulled my trousers down a bit." He stopped there, looking at his friend's face, seeing the longing growing in his small blue eyes. "I was so hard man, it was throbbing. But then they just stood there, looking at it, saying to each other 'You do it', 'No, you do it'. But none of them done it. They just laughed. Fucking bitches."

"They laughed?"

"Yeah, giggling like mad. Y'know I bet that's the first time they ever saw one and that's why they didn't know what to do. Billy Jones. What a fucking liar."

"Yeah, maybe..." Louis said, sitting down on one of the up-turned buckets that the two boys used as seats in their little den. "Or maybe Billy just..."

"Maybe Billy just what?" Jonathan stood defensively and looked at his friend, his eyebrows meeting over his nose.

"Well, maybe Billy just has a better one than you."

"Shut up man, Billy doesn't even have pubes yet."

"How do you know that?" Louis looked confused, trying to think of an answer to how Jonathan would have seen what Billy was packing when he'd been trying and failing for ages.

"Saw it, didn't I. At the cross country race at Easter. When we were getting changed. Tinchy thing. And no pubes. Not like mine."

Louis laughed and stood up, a small bulge visible through his shorts, noticing how Jonathan's eyes lingered on it as he rubbed it with the palm of his hand. "Want me to do it then?"

"Yeah," Jonathan said, already pulling his trousers down, his penis erect once again. "But gimme the magazine, I don't like looking at your face when you're doing it. You always look like you're enjoying it too much. And be quick. I need to go home for my dinner at four."

"Alright, but you need to do mine after," Louis said, pulling the magazine out from under the small mattress that they had brought down the first day they built their den and handing it to Jonathan. He pulled his own trousers down and they lay on the mattress beside each other, their legs touching.

"Don't I always?" Jonathan flicked through the magazine until he got to his favourite pair of tits, waiting for his friend to take it in his hand and start stroking, wishing that it was one of the Hartigan twins instead of him, but accepting that this would have to do for today, grateful that Louis just does it and doesn't laugh, grateful that they are a similar size. Though he doesn't like how much his friend seems to enjoy it or how quickly he always seems to finish, getting it all over his hand before he can pull it out of the way. But he endures it. "Just hurry up though, it's not gonna stay hard forever."

A RETURN TO WHAT YOU DO BEST

A bead of sweat trickled down the side of Emmeline's face, travelled along the sharp edge that was her jaw and threatened to drop onto her new fuchsia coloured yoga mat. But she raised a weary hand and wiped it clear, puffing with exertion in the process. The forty-something-year-old office worker wasn't as fit as she once was. Years ago, in a former life, that no one but she knew about, she would train for hours on end, and never break a sweat. Now, however, ten minutes into a yoga session meant the sweat began to flow. She attributed this partly to 'the change' and partly to the fact she was living a largely sedentary lifestyle now, sitting at a desk from nine 'til five every day, since blagging her way to a new life as the CEO of a publishing firm. Her only means of exercise for the past three years had been her short walk to the subway station and then the even shorter walk to her office once she had ridden the uncomfortably cramped morning train all the way. So, she had decided, since noticing her reflexes had begun to diminish dramatically, that she needed to start up a workout regime again, figuring that yoga would be the easiest way to start.

She was, however, wrong, realising that it required far more athleticism than she first thought. So after ten more minutes of contorting her body into all manner of shapes and positions and a failed attempt at a *Sirsa Padasana*, a head to foot pose that she was struggling to master, Emmeline called it quits. She rolled up her mat, stuffed it back into the paltry closet just off the living room of the small apartment she had recently purchased and decided that she would try again tomorrow.

After she showered and changed into her casuals- a navy blue vest top, baggy grey sweats and a pair of *Nike* running shoes that she had only worn a handful of times- she plucked a CD from amid the pile that she had amassed and which had now grown to such a height that it now teetered precariously beside her digital stereo. She chose *Summer Rain* by Jeanette Harris this time. A bit of Smooth Jazz. A recent favourite of hers and perfect for a Sunday afternoon after some yoga.

As the sound of saxophones and pianos resonated throughout the sixth floor Manhattan apartment that Emmeline inhabited alone, she began to prepare a meal for herself. She'd always had a passion for cooking, but her life prior to becoming CEO of Gardiner and Sons did not allow her any time to pursue this specific avenue. Now, however, she was getting a chance to hone her cheffing skills and there was a vast array of cookbooks scattered throughout the apartment. From *The Taste of Country Cooking* by Edna Lewis to *The Essentials of Classic Italian Cooking* by Marcella Hazan, there wasn't a cookbook that couldn't be found somewhere in Emmeline's apartment, each one dog eared and bookmarked onto recipes that she wished to try.

As she was turning the page and beginning to scan over the next line of her current Chicken Katsu recipe, three loud thumps rent the air, drowning out the sound of the jazz still sweeping around the apartment. Her heart jumped into her mouth, bouncing off her uvula and the knife, that she was using to dice spring onions, went cascading to the floor. She cursed herself for failing to catch it, for letting herself become startled.

There was another barrage of thumps on the door. Louder. Faster. Impatient.

Scooping the knife up from the floor and holding it loosely by her side, she went to the door and wrenched it open, ready to confront the mystery knocker, confident that it wouldn't be Michael. He wouldn't knock so abruptly. And, besides, he never came on a Sunday. Sundays were for family. And Emmeline wasn't family.

But when she had opened it wide and saw who it was, standing there in all his grandeur, instinct kicked in. Immediately her back straightened, her grip on the knife tightened, her stance became one of defense and her face became rigid, devoid of any expression. Images of a former life, in which she had been employed by this man and his sordid company, if you could call it that, began to creep up from the recesses of her mind. Images that she had fought hard to forget, that still sent a chill down her spine and made her hackles rise.

The man looked at her and, without waiting for an invitation into her home, slipped past Emmeline, lithe as anything and made his way into the living room-cum-kitchen-cum-dining room. He scanned the room with one sweeping motion of his head and, determining that it was safe to do so, settled himself on the high backed armchair beside the stereo, placing the dark leather briefcase he was carrying flat onto his knees.

He closed his eyes and bobbed his head gently to the music. When the track stopped and a new song began to play, he beckoned for Emmeline to join him. She stared at him for a moment, saying nothing, noting the same neatly clipped hairstyle, the same finely tailored pin-striped suit and the same seemingly innocuous but insanely deadly briefcase. But she reacted to his instruction as if she were still in his employ and crossed the room in three short strides.

When she had taken a seat opposite him and held the knife in front of her, one hand on the handle, the other hand cradling the blade, the man, sitting serenely, regarded her with mild curiosity for a moment, acknowledging the subtle differences she had made- the new pixie-like haircut, the removal of the shoulder tattoo, the pencilled on eyebrows- before saying simply, as if telling an inquisitive passerby the time: "We found him."

The three little words hung in the air between the two for a long time, the soft jazz still playing on the stereo, the man's hands clasped together on the pristine surface of his briefcase. After some time, in which Emmeline's face seemed to flicker through a series of strained emotions, she rose from her chair, knife still in hand and returned to the kitchen. The man watched, this time not with mild curiosity but with pure bewilderment, as she chopped, stirred and seasoned, continuing to prepare the meal which anyone looking in on this strange scene, would have thought she was actually looking forward to eating.

Eventually, when it seemed as if Emmeline was planning

on ignoring her old boss and one-time lover entirely, he spoke again, the same words as before. "We found him."

She looked up, placed her hands flat on the counter and spoke, venom attached to every word that came out through her gritted teeth. "How did you find *me*?"

"I didn't have to find you, We never lost you, Em. *I* never lost you."

Her eyes widened at this revelation and without a second thought, she grabbed the knife from the counter and launched it at his head. His reflexes were too fast and he raised his briefcase in time, deflecting the knife, sending it crashing into the stereo. There was a hiss, a small bang and the apartment was plunged into silence for what felt like an eternity.

The man stood up then, left his briefcase on the armchair and walked to the woman he knew well, had loved, hated and loved again, admiring how she had reacted, appreciating how quickly she was willing to let her old instincts and years of training by him take over, relishing the wild look that was now in her eyes which he had come to both love and fear in equal measure over the years.

When he was close enough to feel the hot air that flamed from her nostrils, he spoke again, determined to get what he had come to the apartment for. She was their best after all, and they would do whatever it took.

"I know how you feel Em, how much you hate me, how much you hate what we do, what we made you, what we forced you to do. But you must realise, I wouldn't be here if we didn't have something."

He stopped here, allowing his last statement to sink in. He

could see the disbelief etched into Emmeline's face, her obvious reluctance to accept the truth of what he was telling her.

"You're lying. Just like you did when all of this started and you turned me into a... into a..."

"Look at me. I'm here. In front of *you*. Guard *completely* down. I'm not lying. We really have found him, Em, and I promise you, we won't let him slip through our fingers this time."

He moved even closer and took her hands into his, brought his lips up to the side of her face, and hovered just a hair's breadth away from her ear, his whisper just barely audible over the sound of blood now rushing through her skull, her thoughts a swirling vortex of chaos, memories and love. "So, it's time. For you to come back. To return to what you do best. You need to do this for your son, Em. You need to kill again."

SOMETHING I WOULD GUARD WITH MY LIFE

I still remember the day my father brought it home from the shop. My mother and I stood at the window of our small semi-detached house, watching through the net curtains as he pulled up outside. My fingers twitched, pulling at a loose thread on the netting, as the Ford Cortina stuttered to a halt on the asphalt outside. We watched, breath held, as he stepped out, glanced up the driveway towards the house and made his way to the rear of the car. He popped open the trunk, reached inside and produced an enormous box. He struggled with it for a moment, threatening to overbalance, but he placed it on the ground and snapped the trunk closed with a bang.

I bounced up and down on the balls of my feet, excitement crackling through my veins, electricity buzzing at my fingertips. I couldn't bear to stay at the window, silently waiting for him to pick the box back up. So I raced out into the hall past my mother, slipping on the linoleum and almost colliding with the spindly-legged table upon which the old rotary telephone balanced precariously. I straightened myself up and yanked the door open, my heart threatening to burst out through my chest and land at my father's feet as he made his way towards me. A smile almost as big as mine poked out from under the thick bristles of his moustache.

"Calm yourself lad, it's 'ere now," he had said to me, taking careful steps up the driveway, trying not to lose his footing, as the box wobbled in his arms.

"I know, I know. I just can't believe it. All of my friends are gonna be sooooo jealous. Can I call them now? Tell them to come over? Can I? Can I?"

"Hows about we just wait for a bit lad, eh? At least until we can enjoy it for ourselves first. Before the 'ole street starts showing up. And you know well they will lad, as soon as they find out we 'ave this in the 'ouse. First on the street, maybe even in the 'ole town y'know. Now move out the way and let me inside. This thing is a lot 'eavier than it looks."

I moved aside but followed close at his heels, bobbing my head from side to side, trying to see past his pointed elbows to get another look at the box. I had never seen a box like it- the shapes and colours so vibrant, so inviting, so tantalizingly pleasing- at least never in my own house. I had, of course, seen similar ones in the shop window on the high street every time we passed it on our weekly excursions. And, each time, I had stopped, pressed my face up against the glass, my eyes wide, my grin even wider and asked "When can we get one?" And my father had always replied, "Soon lad, soon."

I must have asked a hundred times or more but his response was always the same. But now... now we finally had one. In our little house in Peckingham. And it was the first on the street he had said, maybe even in the whole town. It was going to change *everything*.

I watched as my father placed the box on the threadbare carpet floor in the lounge, just in front of the settee. When it was free of his touch, he plonked himself down in his armchair just across from it, letting out a long sigh and massaging his lower back. "Be needin' a cuppa now after that, Angela, 'eavier than it seems, y'know."

My mother, however, remained standing at the window, as if afraid to venture anywhere near the box, like it was some strange creature my dad had picked up on the roadside, slammed down on the kitchen table and announced that it was to be that evening's dinner. Eventually, she took a tentative step towards it, peering down her nose at the top of the box, where the two top flaps of brown cardboard were sealed together by a thin strip of clear, perfectly shiny Cellotape.

"I'm not so sure about this Nigel. It's rather big isn't it," my mother had said, smoothing out the front of her pinny, pieces of dried Victoria sponge cake mix flaking off and dropping onto the carpet. "It's going to take up a lot of space."

"Stop frettin' Angela, it will fit perfectly in the corner there." He pointed over beside the large record player that we had inherited from my Uncle Jim a few years previously when he had died unexpectedly. "And the man in the shop told me he has had one in his 'ouse for two months now and swears blind it's the best thing he's ever brought 'ome."

"Well of course the man in the bloody shop is going to say that, he's trying to sell the blooming things, isn't he!" Her cheeks were reddening, her eyes blinking quickly.

"It will be fine Angela, just you watch. Guaranteed you'll be the first one sitting in front of it in the evenings if Danny lad here doesn't beat you to it." He laughed and winked at me, but my mother wasn't impressed and continued to stare at it with apprehension.

"Oh, the dishes are going to just magically wash themselves while I sit staring at this monstrosity are they?"

My dad sighed and started to respond but she dismissed him with a curt wave of her hand and scurried past the box, regarding it with a look of sheer disapproval. She headed straight into the kitchen and within seconds I heard the wireless being switched on and the sound of a drawer being opened and closed aggressively. I knelt down beside the box then and ran my finger along the strip of Cellotape, feeling the smoothness of it under my skin.

"Can we open it now, Dad, please?"

"Of course lad, just do it gentle-like. I don't want any damage done when it's only in the 'ouse ten minutes. H'expensive piece of equipment, that, Danny lad."

I picked at the corner of the tape until it began to lift and peeled it back gently as my father had said to do, the flaps popping apart to reveal the contents within. *Like I'd be anything but gentle anyway*, I had thought as I carefully removed the styrofoam from on top, revealing a shiny, polished wooden surface. I resisted the urge to run my finger along this too, as I had with the Cellotape on top of the box, just in case my hands were not completely clean. This was going to change my life. This was going to make me the absolute envy of all my friends. This was going to make our family the most popular family in town. So this was not something I would treat frivolously. No, this was something I would guard with my life.

My father rose from his chair as I pulled out the last piece of protective styrofoam. He ushered me out of the way and, as if transporting the world's most delicate jewels, lifted the set from its packaging and placed it in the corner nearest the window. I moved forward into a cross-legged position, placing my elbows on my knees, cupping my chin with both hands and peered through his legs as he unravelled the long, black wire.

He gave a slight, approving nod of his head as he examined the plug before, ever so gently, pushing it into the socket on the wall beside him. I leaned forward as he flipped the switch at the front to the 'ON' position. The excitement coursed through my veins, threatening to propel me up from the floor like a rocket shooting off into space.

It took a couple of moments to warm up. Moments that seemed to last hours. Moments in which I thought it was never going to power on. Moments in which I held my breath and thought silently that my father should bring it back to the man in the shop and tell him that he had sold us a dud. But eventually it did come on, the screen flickering, the static crackling, the television set finally coming to life.

THE BOYS WENT INTO THE WOODS TODAY

William "Billy" Jones Junior dangled from the monkey bars, first with both hands, then with only one, his legs drawn up underneath him so that he wouldn't sway too much. He wanted to test himself, to see how long he could last, to ascertain exactly how long his newly built up biceps and triceps could hold up the weight of his recently sculpted body.

After a short while, that was in all actuality only two or three minutes, but that he would later claim was "at least twenty minutes fellas", he felt his fingers start to loosen around the horizontal metal bar. He tried to react quickly, to arc his left arm up but it was too late and the tips of his cigar like fingers just brushed the underside of the bar and he found himself falling a few feet through the air. He landed flat on his back, though he wasn't hurt, the soft, wood chippings scattered throughout the ground of the playground breaking his fall. He swore loudly and stood up quickly, brushing himself off, straightening himself up, not wanting to appear dishevelled when his mates Rocko and Collins arrived.

He didn't have to wait long, seeing Rocko's gangly posture appear over the summit of the small hill, that was really just a raised mound of earth more than an actual hill, his overlarge feet sloping along in front of him. Collins followed a few steps behind, his short legs working double speed just to keep up with his lanky mate. They drew level with Billy at the playground and Rocko greeted him with a fist bump while Collins wrapped his arm around the nearest vertical pole, trying to hide the fact he was panting heavily from the other two.

Billy knew Collins hated being the unfit one of the trio, and he knew that Collins was even more jealous of him now that he had beefed up, while he was still carrying what his mother referred to as "puppy fat". But the three misfit mates rarely spoke of it amongst themselves and never referred to the fact that, at sixteen years old, your "puppy fat" should be well and truly gone. No, the conversations of this group of mates usually revolved around sex, drinking and who was able to score the best weed.

Today though, sex and drugs were the last things on their late adolescent minds as they discussed the recent shocking development that had rocked their small town. Usually, the only scandals that hit the front pages of the local newspapers around their town involved the local football teams' selection criteria and whether the potholes at the end of Shrewsbury road would be fixed by the council before Halloween. This one was different though. This one had shaken the entire community and had sent the townspeople into a frenzy of wild accusations and finger-pointing. A young boy, just twelve years old, had gone missing two days prior. And, by all accounts, the police had done nothing to help, not even bothering to search the nearby woods.

"Probably some pedo got him." Rocko took a long drag from his blunt, then leaned his head back and blew the smoke up into the air, creating a thick cloud above his face that drifted off in the breeze, disappearing a few seconds later. "Y'know, has him chained up to use whenever he wants or something."

"Nah, I reckon he got hit by a car and someone is after hiding the body."

"I think you're both wrong." Billy held out his hand for Rocko to pass the blunt and accepted it between his outstretched fingers. He turned towards the railings at the back end of the playground which faced the nearby woodland. "I think he's in there somewhere and that we should go looking for him."

Collins and Rocko looked dubious and Collins sniggered a little. "Come off it man, don't be stupid. There's no way. I'm sticking with my theory that he was hit by a car and someone dumped his body."

"Is it though? Stupid? Think about it, Collins," said Billy, turning back around to face his mates, taking a long drag from the shrinking blunt. The smoke poured out of his mouth as he continued to speak. "Let' say even if he was hit by a car and he was dumped. Where would be the most likely place to dump him? In there, right? And the police are doing nothing really. They haven't gone anywhere near there. Sooo... what if we find him? We'll be fucking famous man. We'll be able to pick any pussy we want."

Billy looked from Collins to Rocko, seeing the sides of their mouths beginning to twitch, smiles starting to spread as they pictured, in their minds, their own faces on the front of the papers, the girls at school fawning over them, the football lads wanting to hang out with them: the misfits turned local heroes who had found the missing schoolboy.

"Alright, alright, fuck it, let's do it." Rocko took an excited step forward and stood shoulder to shoulder with Billy, facing Collins, who looked hesitantly towards them, his two front teeth picking at the loose, dead skin on his bottom lip.

"Come on Collins, think about all the pussy you will get."

"You will have your pick Collins, any pussy you want." Billy cupped and pulled at his crotch, making humping motions in Collins' direction. "Probably even Suzie Mulligan will wanna fuck you man."

That idea seemed to clinch it for him, and the thought of pulling up the skirt of Suzie Mulligan, getting her up on his lap and feeling her tight pussy wrapped around his small cock, made him happy.

A smile spread across his face. "Okay. I'm in."

***

Half an hour later the three teenage boys, who were very much sitting on the precipice of adulthood, making their way out of their final years of being called teenagers, stumbled through the thick undergrowth and fallen leaves that made up the ground of the forest. Collins was struggling to keep up with Billy and Rocko, who both seemed to be storming ahead, Billy in the lead, as always. The three of them were keeping their eyes peeled for any evidence that anyone had passed through, or that Sam, the schoolboy who had gone missing two days previous was here, somewhere.

"Yo, Billy." Collins tried to call after the burly leader of the pack, but he was too far ahead to hear him so he took a deep breath in and shouted, his voice echoing throughout the trees, almost making the leaves shudder. "Billy!"

Billy and Rocko turned immediately and Rocko, thinking that the shortest and least imposing member of the trio had spotted something important, raced back, while Billy just wandered back slowly, rolling his eyes, knowing that they were unlikely to find anything around this part of the forest. They were only a few hundred yards in. If it were that simple, he would have been found already.

"What is it? Did you find something?" Rocko looked all around them, his eyes searching the mulchy forest floor.

"Of course he didn't, the fat fucker just needs a break. Right?" Billy raised his eyebrows at Collins who looked away, almost ashamedly.

"Well, yeah, but just for a sec."

Rocko looked disappointed as Collins pulled at the neck of his t-shirt, flapping it in and out, trying to force some air inside to cool his sweaty, oversized chest.

"What are we even looking for exactly?" Rocko leaned up against a tree and stuffed his hands into the pockets of his hoodie. He and Collins looked to Billy as they always did, expecting him to have the answers.

"Dunno really, just anything sort of... not normal I suppose.

Now can we get moving again, fatso?"

Collins looked like he would rather stay where he was a little longer, but he nodded anyway, reluctant to give Billy any more opportunities to insult him.

As they walked on quickly again they stayed in tighter formation, Collins doing everything he could to keep up, Bily leading again, almost seeming like he knew exactly where he was heading, taking deliberate steps towards a final destination.

"Do either of you even know this Sam guy that's gone missing?" Rocko asked, looking from Billy to Collins.

"I think I seen him around at school a few times. Small, little blonde fucker."

"Yeah, I think I seen him a few times too," Collins said. "Well, I recognised his picture when it was on the news this morning anyway."

"Same. But it's freaky though, isn't it? I mean, a kid going missing around here. I really bet it is some pedo that's got him."

Billy shot Rocko a harsh look. "Are you fucking obsessed with pedos or something, man? That's all you seem to be talking about today. I'm telling you it wasn't a fucking pedo, there's no pedos in-"

He stopped mid-sentence, coming to a standstill, his eyes having spotted something in the distance. "What's that fellas?"

Rocko craned his neck. "Dunno, looks like a big rock or something."

Collins looked past his friends' shoulders, squinting his eyes. "I don't see anything."

"There, look." Billy stretched his arm out and pointed. Collins followed with his eyes, looking past the tip of his thick finger.

"Oh, yeah, it looks like a rock or something," Collins said apprehensively, echoing Rocko's earlier assumption.

"Maybe, but look on top, that looks like something doesn't it? Come on." Billy moved ahead quickly, the other two falling in behind him.

When they had rushed forward to the spot that Billy had pointed to only seconds previously, they found themselves emerging into a sort of small clearing, an open area amongst the trees, where there was in fact a large rock, a boulder type thing about six foot in diameter, almost central but not quite. And something was resting on top of it as Billy had thought. A kind of white, plastic tarpaulin. It seemed to cover the entire top surface of the rock, rising in a small dome in the middle, as if something was positioned underneath it, while the edges splayed out, touching the rim of the large rock. It was surprising, too, that it was staying there motionless. Though perhaps, as there were so many trees in the immediate surrounding area, no wind was able to penetrate the small clearing, no sharp gusts able to make their way in and shift the plastic. So, it remained there atop the rock, still and unmoving.

"What do you reckon fellas? Is that something kind of not normal?" Billy asked quietly, edging towards the mysterious appearance, taking slow, careful steps, his two friends falling in behind him.

"That is definitely something not normal." Rocko's voice was soft, almost a whisper.

"Yeah, this doesn't feel right," said Collins his voice sounding strained and choked, like he was scared but trying to feign bravery. "We should go back and tell someone, let them check it out."

"Don't be such a wuss, we can check it out ourselves."

Billy was almost within touching distance of the rock, but he stopped when Rocko spoke. He turned around to look into his friend's face, his eyes steely with determination.

"I dunno Billy, man, m-maybe Collins is right. I don't have a good feeling about this. M-maybe we should get someone, an adult or something, let them have a look first."

"Jesus, when did you two become such wusses? Eh? You two can leave if you want, but I'm gonna check it out myself." He turned back to face the rock and waited for a moment, to see if they would actually walk away. But he knew, really, that if he was staying, they would stay too.

So, knowing that both of their eyes were trained on the back of his head, waiting, he reached out his hand and gripped the edge of the tarpaulin. He gave a rough yank and it came away easily, obscuring their vision of the rock for a few seconds as it flapped and then settled, floating on the air, drifting to the ground, revealing the horror that lay on top of the rock.

Rocko swayed dangerously, threatening to fall over, but he hunkered down, wrapping his arms firmly around his legs, eyes wide. Collins turned away holding his stomach, heaving loudly as bile and vomit coursed up through his oesophagus and splattered out onto the forest floor. Billy however, stared, transfixed at the mutilated body of Sam Prowse, taking in every detail of the bloated skin, marvelling at the large hole through which the top of his white skull was now protruding, smiling as his eyes came to rest on what was once a prepubescent chest but which was now a feeding ground for slimy, bulbous maggots.

"Shit, I wish I had my camera with me." Billy spoke quietly to himself, a little while later, after they had all regained their composure and were standing in a line, staring at the mutilated remains in front of them.

Rocko looked to Billy, a mixture of confusion and disgust clouding his face. "I didn't know you had a camera."

"Yeah, my gran bought it me for Christmas last year. I've only used it once so far. But I wish I had it now."

"Why the fuck would you wanna take a picture of this?"

"Dunno, just weird innit."

"Yeah but, man, that's just sick wanting to take a picture of this. I mean he's completely fucking messed up. How could you even say something like that?"

"Alright, fuck sake, I was just saying…" Billy lapsed into silence, pursing his lips and regarding Rocko with a look of total derision.

"I think we need to tell the police he's here," Collins mumbled, speaking up for the first time since they stumbled upon the body of Sam. He still sounded choked, his voice cracking, his cheeks tear-stained.

"Yeah, alright." Rocko turned away first, followed quickly by Collins, who for the first time in his life seemed set to overtake his gangly mate.

Billy lingered for a moment, the corner of his mouth twitching, as he savoured the warm sensation that was spreading throughout his body.

***

Hours later, after police officers and sniffer dogs had swarmed the forest and surrounding areas, after the three boys had been questioned endlessly about their gruesome discovery, after their parents had brought them home from the local police station one by one, Billy entered his small box room, feeling like he could conquer the world. He was, in his mind, now going to be a celebrity.

He got down onto his knees and reached in under his bed until his hand came to rest on the box he was looking for. He pulled it out, stood up and placed it on top of his bed, the weight of it making a small divet in the duvet cover. He took the lid off slowly, looking at the contents- his camera, a brown envelope and a small, hardcover school yearbook from the previous academic year.

He took the camera out, a Polaroid One Step+. The one his grandmother had bought him for Chrismas, in the hopes that he would take more pictures of the family get-togethers. But, with Billy being Billy, he hadn't spared much thought for it and it had gone unused until two days ago when he had rediscovered it and brought it down to the playground, wrapped in a small white tarp that he had found in his grandfather's shed a few weeks before school ended, which he thought he and his mates could put to good use.

Until he saw Sam sitting on one of the swings by himself

and an entirely new plan started to formulate in his mind.

Now he hung it around his neck, the nylon strap sitting comfortably against his skin. He picked up the large brown envelope next and walked slowly over to his desk. He emptied the contents, photographs, out onto the hard wooden surface and arranged them in the chronological order in which they had been taken and dispensed from the camera. A timeline of events if you will.

He looked at each photograph in turn, admiring his own handiwork, admiring how, with each passing photo, Sam's body became increasingly desecrated and how the light in the young boy's eyes seemed to dim until in the last photo all that was left was a bloody mess and a lifeless face. By the time he reached the last photo, his cock had become fully erect and he could feel it pulsing against the fabric of his trousers.

He picked up the photograph, lay down atop the covers of his bed, nudging the box out of the way. He undid his trousers and let his cock spring out, the stiffness of it becoming uncomfortable, almost painful. But he closed his eyes, bringing the photograph up to rest against his lips and gripped it with his free hand, making long gentle strokes, his body squirming while the camera bounced up and down lightly on his chest.

When it seemed like he was about to finish, Billy's eyes snapped open. He sat up and stuffed his penis back into his boxer shorts. He reached into the box that was beside him and extracted the final object in there. A school yearbook, that everyone had received a copy of during the final week of school last term. He turned to the page that he had dog eared after leaving the body on top of the rock the other day and looked at the photograph of class C12. He smiled as his eyes came to rest on Sam, standing innocently in front of the teacher, Miss Riley, a red halo now encircling his smiling face, etched onto the shiny surface of the photograph.

Then, as he brought the open yearbook over to his desk, he lifted the red pen, touched it to the page and drew another circle around a beaming face, the inky red line cutting through the tips of Annabelle Morgan's pigtails.

A PROPOSAL OF TRUTH

"Would you like another drink while you wait for your gentleman friend to arrive?"

Sarah didn't register the voice speaking to her and continued to stare at the unlocked screen of her phone, her fingers drumming mindlessly on the table beside it, creating a steady rhythm akin to a cluster of beating hearts. The time on the phone showed 7:57 pm. The dinner had been scheduled for seven-thirty. Yet there was still no text from Paul, no indication that he was on his way.

She'd arrived early, taken her seat at the well laid out table and began to rehearse in her head the exact words she could use to lessen the impact of the bomb she was about to drop straight into their lives. But he was now almost half an hour late. And that wasn't like Paul at all. He hated to be late for anything, hated to show up even five minutes after he was supposed to be somewhere and loathed when anything went over time and pushed his plans out of kilter.

So did that mean he knew? About that night she spent with Simon? Was this his idea of payback? Was he going to leave her sitting there, alone, waiting? Was it his plan to humiliate her, to belittle her, to make her feel even just an ounce of the anger that he would surely be feeling if he really did know?

"Madam?" The waiter smiled thinly through gritted teeth, his frustration starting to grow at having to prompt her yet again.

"Paul?"

Sarah's head snapped up from her phone and a faint smile began to cross her face at the sound of the voice but fell away swiftly when she saw that it wasn't him, that it was just the waiter. His growing frustration began to ebb away then, as he saw the expectant look on her face and he smiled at her softly, knowing. He'd seen this scenario unfold many times.

"Yes?"

"Would you like another drink while you wait?" His eyes moved in the direction of the empty glass that had contained the water he had brought her almost thirty minutes earlier.

"Oh, er, no thank you. I'm just waiting for my, er, friend."

He smiled and gave a slight nod before picking up the glass and turning away. Sarah watched him as he headed for the kitchen, noticing how the tight black trousers he wore rubbed against his firm buttocks with each stride. That reminded her of the first time she saw Simon, how she couldn't help but stare as he bent down to pick up the papers he had dropped...

She shook her head and glanced around the restaurant briefly, before looking down at her phone again. 8:02 pm. With a quiet sigh of resignation, she leaned forward and picked up her bag from the floor, careful not to compress her stomach too much, the waistband of her trousers beginning to feel taut against her expanding midriff. Though the blouse she wore did a good job of hiding that.

She was beginning to stand, her buttocks just hovering above the navy fabric of the chair, when she heard footsteps approaching behind her. The waiter back again, she thought. But a hand came to rest on her shoulder and she settled back into a sitting position, a breathless voice making its way to her ear. "So sorry I'm late darling. Absolute dickheads in the office held me up. Drink?"

Paul took the seat opposite her across the small, finely laid table. His forehead was sweaty. His chest rose and fell rapidly and his hands seemed to tremble slightly.

"What are you having?" He asked, twisting in his seat, looking around for the waiter.

"Nothing, thank you. I've had one already. While I was waiting. You could have texted me. I was just about to leave."

"Yes, well, I seem to have misplaced my phone, sorry about that." He shifted his weight around in the chair and his foot tapped rapidly under the table. He resisted the urge to reach in, take it out right then and wave the small box in front of her face. But he didn't want to ruin the surprise. Not yet. "But no worries. I'm here now."

He leaned across the table and kissed her. His lips trembled a little. But she didn't notice. She kissed him back, happy, for the briefest moment, that he was here. But that wouldn't last. When she told him what she had to tell him, that happiness would be gone. Ripped from their lives because of one stupid mistake. A mistake called Simon.

"Are you alright darling? You don't look too well."

"Yes, yes, I'm fine."

"You're sure? We can take a rain check on dinner if you'd rather head home? We can curl up in front of the TV. Watch that show you were telling me about last week."

"No, no, not at all, I'm fine."

"Great, okay, well as long as you are happy, I am happy." He smiled at her, thinking about just doing it, getting it over with, so that the nerves, that were such an unnatural and alien feeling to him, would dissipate. "Now where's the waiter? I'm parched."

Paul smacked his lips together and twisted in his chair again and when he spotted the young man tending to an elderly, white-haired couple, he gestured for him to come over.

"Ah, I see your gentleman friend has finally arrived," he said to Sarah as he approached the table. "What can I get the lovely couple this evening?"

"I'll start with a bottle of your house ale for myself and a-" Paul looked first at Sarah, then down at the glass free table that sat between them, faltering a little.

"Just a water please."

"And just a water for my beautiful girlfriend."

"Very well and will you be ordering food this evening?"

"Yes, I think we will," Paul said, his hand reaching up to touch the breast pocket of his dinner jacket. This movement went unnoticed by Sarah, who was beginning to pale, the moment in which she must admit everything fast approaching.

"Thank you, sir. One ale, one water and two menus coming right up."

"Thank you."

"I wonder if they have any lobster left..." Paul said craning his neck to look at the surrounding tables to see what the people sitting at them were eating, scowling when he saw what appeared to be a full rainbow trout two tables over.

"Paul?"

"I haven't had a nice lobster since that weekend in Milan. Maybe I'll try the steak instead. Can't go wrong with a good steak. Though that calamari the gentleman over there is eating looks delicious."

"Paul?"

"What do you think darling, lobster or steak?"

"Paul!"

The people at the surrounding tables looked up at the sound of the raised voice.

Paul smiled at them, brushing it off, leaning forward and speaking quietly to Sarah now. "What's wrong, darling? Are you feeling okay? I said we could go if you're not feeling well. We can do this another night. You don't look very we-"

"Paul. Stop. Just shush. There's something I need to tell you. It's abou-"

The waiter came with the drinks and placed a leather-bound menu flat on the table in front of both Sarah and Paul. Sarah looked impatiently at Paul as he thanked the waiter and she barely registered the voices of the two men as they discussed the day's specials.

The waiter noticed, as he regurgitated for the hundredth time that evening what the specials were, the look on her face as she watched the man in front of her, her right hand now gripping the menu, her left hand resting on her stomach. He noticed the sweat on the man's forehead and how he patted the breast pocket of his jacket, his foot tapping to an invisible beat.

"I'll give you a little longer to decide," he said, quickly backing away from the table, knowing only too well, that these people, each with their own agenda for being there, were not going to be eating that evening.

THE BAD DEAL

1.

"**I** don't want to go." I cross my arms in front of my chest and scrunch up my face. I kick my legs out and they hit the back of Daddy's seat. But he doesn't mind because he knows, just like I do, that it's not comfortable being in the car. It's just way too warm.

'Sticky weather' is what Grandpa calls it when it is like this. When you just have to have a big cold glass of lemonade. With three lumps of ice. Because two is not enough and four would just be way too many. Well, that's what Grandpa says and Grandpa is always right. Always. You know, I wish we were going to his house instead, but Mammy says it's too far away. Hmpfh! Like she would even know, she's not even the one driving the car!

I have to keep wiggling my bum around to stop my legs sticking to the leather in Daddy's car. But my shorts keep making a funny scrapey sound when they rub against the hot leather. Mammy turns around in her seat to look at me properly when she's talking. I see the seatbelt disappearing behind her big fat belly every time she does that.

"You have to go sweetheart. Daddy and I have a meeting with very important people. Uncle Clem will take good care of you."

"But... but...Uncle Clem is boring. He doesn't even have a TV, Mammy! And why does it have to be for the WHOLE weekend?"

Daddy looks up into the mirror so he can see me sitting in the back. I look into his big eyes and he looks into mine. His are blue. Just like mine. Not like Mammy's ugly green eyes. And Mammy always says we have the same eyes. But that doesn't mean they're exactly the same, you know, because if we had the exact same eyes only one of us would be able to see. It's just that they look a bit the same. And I'm glad. I don't want to have stupid green eyes like her. Bleh!

Daddy smiles at me. One that's big and wide and shows all of his teeth. A Daddy smile, meant only for me. He doesn't even say anything. He doesn't need to. I know that if he is smiling then everything is going to be *okey dokey*. I don't need to be scared. So I unscrunch my face and smile back showing all my teeth, well the ones that the tooth fairy didn't get yet. But I keep my arms crossed. Only because if I put them back by my side they will get stuck to the seat and be all sweaty. Yuck!

I sing my favourite songs and play *I Spy* with Mammy as we drive. I always win. Because I'm better than she is. And through the open windows of the car we see lots of fields filled with cows and sheep. There's even horses in some of them, and beside the big barns there are GINORMOUS bales of hay. I remember when I went to the farm one time with Grandpa and cousin Ginny. She was afraid to jump off the biggest bale of hay. But that's okay, she is only four after all.

But I wasn't afraid. I jumped off it loads of times. And on the last time, Grandpa caught me. He pretended I was really heavy and that he was about to fall but he was just being silly. It was so, so fun. I wish I could do that again. But I can't. Because I have to go and stay with stupid Uncle Clem.

Daddy tells me stories of when him and Uncle Clem were kids. Uncle Clem is Daddy's big brother. He tells me that when they were my age they always went on adventures and one time they went on this big adventure beside the river and that he fell in but Uncle Clem jumped straight in and rescued him. He says it all made Grandma very upset when she found out and that she would always get angry when they went on really long adventures after that.

"But she didn't really get upset," he says, laughing like the way I laugh when I watch *Disney Channel*. "She was just happy as long as we got along and didn't fight all the time. Mainly she just didn't want us to be late for dinner. But we always were. Because we just had to go on adventures!"

He laughs at this and looks at me through the mirror again. He taps his hand on the steering wheel, his long fingers making a doof doof sound when they hit it. "You'll have a great time with Uncle Clem, Kiddo. And it won't be for long. We'll collect you on Sunday and if you've been good for your uncle you can even stay off school on Monday. Deal?"

I nod my head and smile. "Okay, Daddy. Deal." That does sound like a very good deal. And I'm the best at doing deals. My friend Sam says so. He will be so jealous when I tell him about it on Tuesday.

It's nearly dark when we arrive at Uncle Clem's house. The sun is going down behind the trees that are lined up at the front of the garden. The shadows they make on the grass look like soldiers all lined up, ready to go into a big battle. Like in that film Mammy said I wasn't supposed to watch.

We drive through big wooden gates up a long windey path to a big house. It's about twenty bazillion times bigger than ours. And it's all grey and has silly weeds growing up along the front of it over the door. It looks like one of the houses in them old paintings Mammy showed me once. They were horrible.

Daddy turns the car off and gets out of his seat. He opens the door for me and I jump out. My legs wobble a bit and the warm breezy air makes my hair go flippy-flappy around my ears. There's a funny smell. It tickles my nose, making me sneeze one, two, three times.

"Ha! You'll soon get used to the country air," a voice says behind us. It's a deep voice. But not an angry one like Mr. Devine at school.

Uncle Clem is standing in the open door of the house when we turn around. He's tall. Even way more taller than Daddy. His belly is bigger now and his hair is a different colour than I remember. Longer and loads more grey. He's wearing a red checkedy shirt and jeans that have big holes where his knees are and black wellies that are dirty with all dried mud on them. He reminds me of a scarecrow.

He walks over from the door and hugs Mammy ("Great to see you Ange") and shakes Daddy's hand ("Looking tired there, buddy"). Then he bends down and hugs me. His hand rubs up and down my back and he sniffs my hair. And it's a warm hug. Like Daddy's. He probably learned from Daddy how to give hugs. They are brothers after all you know.

He stands up and holds my hand in his. It's chubby and wraps around mine, covering it all up, but it's softer than I thinked it would be. It's like Grandpa's hand but not as wrinkly. And he's not like a scarecrow at all. Not really.

He tells Daddy to get my things from the car and walks with me and Mammy through the loooong hallway to the kitchen. On the way I look into the living room. I see a sofa and two teeny-weeny armchairs around a little table like they are having a tea party. There is a big bookcase the size of the whole wall behind the chairs. And still no TV! Ugh!

There's not much in the kitchen. It's not like our big, shiny one at home. Here it is really old and there are only a few cupboards, a teensy fridge in one corner that only comes up to Uncle Clem's shoulder, a teeny-weeny cooker in the other one. And at the back wall, near the door, is a small, square table. Just two chairs. At home we have six. I sit in one of them, my legs swinging back and forward. Mammy and Uncle Clem stand by the sink.

"Cup of tea for you and himself, Ange?"

"No, thank you, Clem. We won't stay, we have to be getting back. Important meeting early in the morning." She rubs her fat belly and looks at me quickly then back at Uncle Clem.

"Not a problem, Ange. I'm sure it will all be for the best," he says, not looking at Mammy but looking down at his feet, like I do when I get in trouble at school for doing some-thing naughty.

"Yes, er, thank you, Clem."

Everyone is really quiet after that until Daddy comes in

with my bags. Uncle Clem tells him to bring them up to the room I'll be staying in. When he comes back down him and Mammy say goodbye too quickly and they tell me they'll be back on Sunday and that I should be good for Uncle Clem. Daddy even forgot to give me one of his hugs. But it's okay. I will give him a giant hug on Sunday. Because I will do the deal and he always gives me a giant hug when I win our deals.

We wave at the car as it drives away back down the long driveway. Then it's just me and Uncle Clem. In the kitchen. Alone. I don't know what to do so I just sit quietly at the table. The kitchen is very small. But it's very tidy. More tidy than our kitchen at home.

"Well, now, you must be getting hungry," Uncle Clem says to me.

I nod that I am.

"Bit shy, are we?"

I start to nod again but I'm not shy, not really, so I do a little shrug instead.

"Ha! Well, that will soon be fixed. There's no shyness allowed in this house. Everyone here has to be loud and fun. That's one of the rules!"

He takes some sausages out of the fridge. Then he takes a loaf of bread and a butter dish like Grandma's from the cupboard over the sink. From the one beside that he takes out two plates and from a drawer, that goes like SZSZSZSZ when he opens it, he takes out a knife. He cuts two thick slices of bread from the big loaf that is as big as my head and butters them. Then he puts some sausages in the pan and they sizzle, like in the song, *Ten fat sausages sizzling in a pan, one goes pop and the other goes-*

"We'll get you a bath after you eat," he says to me, turning the sizzling sausages over in the pan and making me forget the song I'm singing in my head. "It was very warm out today, wasn't it? And being in the car for so long you must be sticky with the sweat. And we always need to be clean. That's a rule here too!"

I nod.

"What's that? Remember the first rule? Loud."

"Er, yes, thank you, Uncle Clem," I say, making my voice loud and doing my manners like Grandma teaches me.

When the sausages are cooked and we're eating them he asks me questions about Mammy and Daddy. He asks do I know where they're going. I tell him I don't because they didn't tell me. He asks do I know why Mammy is getting fat. I tell him I don't. He asks do I know why Daddy is looking tired these days. I tell him I don't. But I don't think Daddy is looking tired. He is just looking like the way he always looks.

"Good," he says and when he opens his mouth I can see bits of sausage and bread in his teeth. Ew! "What adults do is their business. They are always right and they should always be respected, even if you think they're doing wrong. That's another rule. Remember that!"

"Okay, I will remember."

Uncle Clem has lots and lots of rules. Be loud. Always be clean. Respect adults even if they're doing wrong things. That's too many. And they're all silly. But I will remember them. And I will follow them. Because I have to do the deal with Daddy. I have to win.

I finish eating and when the only thing left on the plates is my crusts he takes my plate and puts it into the big white sink. He claps his hands together and the noise sounds like one of my toy guns at home.

"Now, then, bath time. Lets's go get nice and clean."

He takes my little hand in his big chubby one again and we go upstairs, into the bathroom. The bath is HUGE. I bet like two Uncle Clems could fit in it and he's really, really big! He turns on the taps at the end and hot water comes shooting out. I know it's hot because I can see a bit of steam going floaty up into the air. But I hope it's not too hot because I'm already sweaty and I don't want to get more sweaty! When it's full about halfway up he kneels beside the bath and picks up a sponge.

"Come on then, let's get you washed."

"I can wash myself." I hold my hand out for the sponge and look towards the door, waiting for him to leave.

"Well that's okay, you can wash yourself, but I'll stay anyway. Just to make sure you clean yourself properly." He throws the sponge into the bath and it floats on top of the water.

Why does he want to stay? Mammy doesn't stay anymore when I wash myself at home. She just leaves the door open and talks to me from her and Daddy's bedroom. We sometimes play a game where we each sing a line of a song and if we forget what line is next we have to start over. I'm always better than Mammy. She forgets all the time.

"Well, go on then. Take off your clothes and get in." Uncle

Clem gets up off his knees, closes the door and sits on the toilet that is in front of the bath. "Remember what the first rule is. There's no shyness allowed in this house!"

I stand beside the bath, feeling all confused. But I have the deal with Daddy to be good. And I need to do that deal because I'm the best at deals. And I don't want to be afraid either. So I take off my clothes, taking off my shoes first, then my t-shirt and shorts. When I take off my undies Uncle Clem leans forward and smiles. I'm starting to feel a bit shy now. But I keep going, finally taking off my socks. The tiles are cold under my feet so I wiggle my toes up and down and then climb over the side of the bath quickly. The water *is* warm but not too warm. It's just nice.

His eyes look at me all over as I wash myself. First my chest, then my belly and under my arms where all the smelly sweat lives. When I put the sponge down under the water to wash my privates I see Uncle Clem move forward on the toilet. He holds his breath like he is going to do a dive into a big swimming pool like when you go on holidays and his eyes go big and the top of his tongue licks his lips. I wash it quickly and then finish up. I put the sponge on the side of the tub and take the big black stopper out. I pull my legs up to my chest and watch the water go swish, swish, swish down the hole, making a big glugglugluglug sound when it gets to the end and all the water is sucked down.

I stand up and climb out of the bath, putting my hands over my privates. Uncle Clem grabs a towel from the shelf over the toilet and holds it out. I step forward and he wraps me up in it, rubbing up and down my arms.

"Good. Good. Probably need to be more thorough though. We'll try again tomorrow."

Try what again tomorrow? What did I do wrong? I washed myself the way Mammy showed me. If Uncle Clem wants to teach me a new way he should ask Mammy. But maybe she showed me wrong first. Ugh. She never does anything right! She's so stupid!

We go to the bedroom and Uncle Clem turns on the light. I can see my bags and stuff over by the bedside table. The wallpaper in this room is all old and it is falling off at the edges where the different pieces should be stuck together. The bed has a duvet and two pillows on it. The duvet is grey and stripedy. Ugly. Like something Mammy would choose. But the pillows look big and soft and comfy. He takes my pajamas from the smallest one of my bags and puts them on the bed. He rubs them out like Grandma does when I stay with her. She says it is for "smoothing out the creases". But it's silly really, because I pick them up like two seconds later and then they just get all messy again. Old people do funny things sometimes.

"Now, here you go. You get changed into them and hop into bed. We'll have an early start in the morning."

I do what he says, dressing very fast because I don't want to be naked around Uncle Clem anymore. I put my head down on the pillow and pull the duvet up over my chest, leaving my arms out, because it doesn't feel nice when they're all tucked in. The pillow is very comfy, but I knew that it would be when I looked at it. Uncle Clem stands beside me, smiling. He reaches his hand out and rubs my hair. It goes in between his chubby fingers. His tongue goes out between his lips again, like it did when he was watching me in the bath.

"Well, goodnight, don't let the bed bugs bite!"

He bends and puts his lips against my head. A kiss. Like Mammy does every night at bedtime. But this is different. It's weird. It is lasting too long. I can feel his lips getting all warm on my skin. I can feel his body shaking as he takes a deep breath in. Finally, he stands up all the way, rubs my face with the back of his chubby fingers and walks out the door, turning the light off as he goes.

I lie in the dark for a while and close my eyes, to try to go asleep but I can't. I don't feel right. Why did he want to stay in the bathroom when I was washing myself? I'm big now. I don't need anyone to stay. Daddy would have told him that. Daddy would have told him that I can do loads of things by myself now. I'm not a baby anymore. I'm not like cousin Ginny. I'm not four! And why did he kiss me like that?

There's a weird feeling inside my belly. Like the feeling I get when I do something bad and Mammy starts to yell at me. I don't like it.

I hear a noise and open my eyes to look at the door. A light comes on outside and shines through the gap under it. I see a shadow getting bigger on the floor through the gap and the little white doorknob starts turning very slow.

My belly feels like I'm going to get sick.

The door opens.

I feel scared.

Uncle Clem comes into the room.

2.

I sit up in bed and rub my eyes with my fingers. The tears are all gone now but they are still stinging. I didn't want to cry. I wanted to be brave and to be good. So that I could still do the deal with Daddy. But it hurt me and I had to cry. And I had to scream too. But Uncle Clem put his hand over my mouth when I did that. It didn't feel warm and chubby on my mouth though. It was sweaty and it made my lips get pushed against my teeth and the sharp bits hurt my mouth. But, when he put my pajamas back on and lied down beside me and snuggled me, his hands were soft again as they rubbed my belly.

And now I have to do the new deal with him. But I won't be able to tell my friend Sam about this one. That is part of it. I can't tell anyone. Because, if I tell anyone, I will lose the deal. He said so. And I can't lose the deal. Because I need to keep being the best at deals. And I need to follow the rules. Because even though Uncle Clem was doing a wrong thing, I need to follow his rules or else he will tell Daddy and then I will lose my deal with him. And I don't want to lose that deal either.

I hear footsteps outside so I lie down quickly and pull the duvet up under my chin. The door opens and Uncle Clem sticks his head around the door. He makes a funny face, sticking out his tongue.

"Good morning Kiddo." He smiles at me. But I don't smile back. Because he called me Kiddo. Only Daddy calls me

Kiddo. Daddy won't be happy at that.

He walks into the room and sits on the edge of the bed. I feel it going down and I almost roll over, but I hold onto the duvet and I stay where I am. He puts his hand on my face and rubs under my eyes with his thumb.

"Oh, look at those red eyes, must be the country air, making them all puffy. And you know, crying doesn't help, so we will have to make sure there's no more crying today, okay. And remember our deal?"

I nod my head a little bit to show him I remember the deal.

"What's that?"

"I remember."

"Good, good." He turns away from me and pats his shoulder. "Hop on, I'll give you a piggyback down for breakfast."

I sit up and push the duvet off me. I climb onto Uncle Clem's back, putting my hands on his shoulders, but he pulls them tight under his chin and it feels spiky, like when Daddy tires to grow a beard and Mammy laughs at him. Then he stands up and we rise up into the air. It is so high being up here. Way higher than when Daddy gives me a piggyback. He puts his elbows around my legs and turns his head so that his nose is pointing out and I can see into his ear. There is lots of white hairs growing in it. EUGH!!!

"Okay, Kiddo, hold on tight, this is gonna be a b-b-b-buuummmpppyyy ride."

Then he is shooting off through the door, running fast, his feet stamping on the floor. He lifts his left leg off the ground and leans back, making a silly noise like a horse. It feels like I am about to fall off so I hold my hands tighter around his neck, but he goes forward and keeps running, bumping me up and down, my head going all wibbly-wobbly.

It is scary but it is really fun as well.

He actually isn't that scary really.

I start to laugh.

***

I don't know why I was so scared. Uncle Clem is really fun. Even though he done a wrong thing last night he is really fun today. After breakfast, he told me to pick whatever I wanted to wear and then he let me get dressed by myself. So I put on my favourite red shorts that Mammy packed in my bag. She forgot my favourite *Ben 10* T-shirt though, so I had to choose one of the yellow ones she put in my bag instead. I hate yellow. Ugh!

But then, when I was dressed and had my shoes on and my laces tied up all by myself in big loopy, swoopy knots the way I like them, Uncle Clem and me played in his GINORMOUS back garden. Seriously it is so big. I wish Grandpa could be here with us. We could play so many good football games here! And I would be able to run and score and do a big celebration and shout out loud as much as I wanted because Uncle Clem says he has no neighbours near, so we wouldn't be disturbing anyone.

That's not like at home. At home when I play in the garden I have to be really quiet because our neighbour, stupid Mrs. Clancy always, always moans when I play too loud. There was one time when me and Sam were playing wrestling on my trampoline and Daddy came out and said we had to stop because Mrs. Clancy couldn't concentrate on her baking because we were being so loud. She is so annoying! Even Mammy thinks she is annoying. I heard her saying it one time. But she didn't know I was listening. I was sneaking that time.

Now Uncle Clem is letting me dig a hole where he says he is going to plant some flowers. I push the little shovel into the muck and flick it up and it goes everywhere. But Uncle Clem says that it is okay if it goes everywhere, even on my clothes and hands because he wants a really big hole. And I'm going to do that for him.

He hasn't even told me any more rules either. But I still remember the three from yesterday. Be loud. Always be clean. Respect adults even if they're doing wrong things. And I am following them. I think. I mean I am being really loud today and I am respecting Uncle Clem even though he did a wrong thing last night but I am not clean. I am all muddy and dirty from digging and playing in the garden all day. But he says it's okay to get muddy so he won't give out to me about that!

Uncle Clem puts all of his tools back into the shed when we are finished planting all of the flowers and then looks at me. His eyes go big and wide and then he starts laughing. "Oh dear lord, look at the dirt of you, Kiddo. Your parents would kill me if they saw how dirty you were. We better get you another bath and get those clothes of yours in the washer. Hop on!"

He gives me another bumpy piggyback ride upstairs and stops outside the bathroom door. It's open and I can see the huge bathtub in there and I remember yesterday and the way it was when Uncle Clem was there when I was cleaning myself. But he is being really fun today and yesterday he didn't know that I am able to wash myself now, because Daddy probably just forget to tell him that I can do lots of things myself now, but I told him and he saw me and now he doesn't have to stay today. It will be better if he doesn't stay.

He puts me down on the floor and we walk into the bathroom. He sits on the toilet like last time, putting his big hands on his knees, where the holes in his jeans are.

"Well, go on then, fill up the bath there, I'm exhausted." He looks at me, and I don't move for like a second but then I do.

"Okay."

I put the stopper in and then turn the taps all the way around until the water starts splishing and splashing down into the tub. When the water is up nearly halfway I turn the taps off and look at Uncle Clem. He just smiles but doesn't leave like I want him to. But I'm not going to tell him because I don't want him to get mad after all the fun we had today. And he might get mad if I ask him to leave. And then I would lose the deal with Daddy. And that can't happen!

I take off all my stinky, muddy clothes and get into the warm water. I sit with my legs crossed, pick up the yellow sponge from the side of the tub and then dip it into the water. I squeeze it tight in my hand and then rub my face with it, all the water dripping down my cheeks. I start to rub my belly with it but Uncle Clem stands up and then kneels beside the bath, putting his hands over the edge and taking the sponge off me.

"Now, remember I said we need to be more thorough,

Kiddo, so look, I'll show you how to do it properly," he says and dips the sponge into the water like I did.

I hold my breath and he puts it on my belly. He rubs it, washing all the dirt off.

"Now, isn't that better?"

What is he talking about? It isn't better. It's exactly the same way I do it. He dips the sponge back into the water and then puts it back on my belly. His hand starts to move down lower. I don't want him to touch it, not like he did last night. But if I start to cry he might put his hand over my mouth and hurt my lips like he did last night. So I just close my eyes. I can think of a song while he is washing it. *Twinkle Twinkle little star*... I can feel the sponge touching it... *How I wonder*... He is starting to rub harder... *What you ar-*

There's a loud bing-bong noise and I forget what line I'm on. Uncle Clem says a bad word and stops washing me.

"Shit!"

I open my eyes and look at him. He drops the sponge and stands up, his eyes all wide like Mr. Owl and his hands are shaking. "Er, right, you stay here, and I'll go see who that is."

I start to say okay but he is already gone out through the door, his footsteps going dum, dum, dum on the hard floor very quickly. The door downstairs at the front of the house opens and I hear someone say "Hello Clem." I don't know who it is. I don't know that voice. But Uncle Clem doesn't say hello back. I just hear the sound of people walking down the long hallway to the little kitchen.

I pick the sponge back up and start to wash myself again

but the voices downstairs are getting louder. It sounds like the time a few weeks ago when Mammy and Daddy were fighting and I could hear them from up in my room and I sneaked out onto the landing and listened to what they were saying. It was something about giving a baby away but I didn't really understand what they were talking about because I'm not a baby anymore and Daddy would not let Mammy give me away. No way!

I take the stopper out of the bath and get out onto the tiles. My feet are slippy but I walk careful and climb onto the toilet. I get a towel and put it over my shoulders, like a superhero cape. Then I walk real slow so that nobody hears me being sneaky. I stand at the top of the stairs. The voices downstairs are really loud now. It sounds like Uncle Clem is having a fight with someone. He sounds really mad. But I still don't know who the other person is. I never heard his voice before. I stay really quiet and listen.

"I've changed my mind. The child is staying here and then going back with my brother and his wife tomorrow."

"Don't tell me you've fallen into your dirty old ways again, Clem. I thought we had curbed those urges. If *she* finds out you have been fiddling with the merchandise again, she-

"There is no merchandise, the deal is off. I have already told you. I will not tell you again!"

There is a loud bang and then lots of noise, like when Grandma's dog Tilly jumped up onto the counter in her house and knocked all the plates down. They smashed on the floor and Grandma got really angry. And there is lots of bad words being said, even worse than the one Uncle Clem said in the bathroom a few minutes ago. I only know they're bad because Mammy shouts at me when I try to say them.

There's one more loud scrapey noise and then a man walks into the long hall. He doesn't look up the stairs but I hide behind the banister anyway, just in case he looks and sees me being sneaky. He has a stripedy suit and he is wearing glasses. He has a briefcase in his hand, like the man on the telly does when he comes out of the door that the policeman has to open. But this man's one is brown, not black like the man on the telly.

"Fine," he says, looking really angry. "We will look elsewhere tonight, only because you have proven to be a useful resource over the years. But be warned, Clem, if you ever back out of a deal again, we will end you. You know we have the power."

He walks to the end of the hallway and goes out through the door at the front of the house. He slams it and I hear Uncle Clem saying a really, really bad word from the kitchen. I don't know what all of that was. Why was that man and Uncle Clem fighting? What did all of that stuff mean? What is mer-chan-dise? And why did he tell Uncle Clem he has power? Uncle Clem is a grown-up. He is bigger and stronger than that man, so he has more power.

I turn around and start to walk back to the bathroom but I hear a noise like really big thunder and then there is a hand grabbing me on my shoulder. I get spinned around and Uncle Clem is standing over me, looking at me.

"How much of that did you hear?" He looks really angry and scary. "I said how much of that DID YOU HEAR? AN-SWER ME!"

My lips starts to go wobbly. "N-n-n-nothing."

"What did you see?"

"I-I-I didn't see anything."

He squeezes my arm really tight. "Oww"

"Shut up!" He drags me and opens the bedroom door. "I told you there would be no more crying!" Now get in there and shut up!"

He pushes me into the bedroom and I fall onto my bum. The towel falls off my shoulders onto the floor and Uncle Clem slams the door shut making my shoulders jump. It is dark but the moon is shining in through the window so I can see a little bit. My pajamas are on the end of the bed, where I left them this morning, so I put them on and climb into the bed. I pull the duvet up over my head. I can feel tears on my cheeks so I stick my head and arms out of the duvet and wipe them off with my hands. I can feel my heart going all bump, bump, bump so I put my hand under the duvet again and hold onto my belly.

I hear loud footsteps outside the door and I can see a shadow under the gap getting bigger. The door opens really hard and hits off the wall making everything shake. I hold onto the duvet really tight under my chin. But Uncle Clem walks in and pulls it out of my hand. I start to cry and scream.

He is going to do the wrong thing again. I try to move away from him but he pulls my leg. I kick him but he holds my two legs down on the bed and I can't move.

I scream louder.

He takes off my pajamas.

3.

Uncle Clem puts butter on my toast and says that I should eat it. I don't want to eat it but my belly is going all rumbly, so I have to. Because Mammy says when your belly goes all rumbly it means that you are hungry and that you should eat something. So that is what I am going to do. Even though I don't want to. And I don't want to stay with Uncle Clem anymore. He does wrong things all the time. He is not fun. He is just a bad old man. I need Daddy to come and get me.

He sits on the chair in front of me and rubs my knee. "Now, Kiddo, do you remember the deal we made?"

I nod but he looks at me and I know what he is going to say, so I swallow the piece of toast in my mouth and do it out loud. "Yes."

My voice is really quiet, my throat feeling all scratchy from screaming so much last night. Like when you have a cold and you sound silly like an old man.

"Good, because, like I said, you can never tell anyone about our secret deal. If you do tell anyone you will lose the deal. And then everyone will hate you. No one will be your friend. And then you won't ever be able to do deals again. Do you understand?"

"Yes."

"Good, now finish eating that toast and go get your stuff all packed up and ready for when your Daddy comes, he will be here soon."

I pack up all of my things, except my pajamas because I can't find them. Uncle Clem probably put them in the washer. But it's okay. I don't even want them anymore. And I don't want to be here anymore. So Daddy better hurry up. Uncle Clem brings all my bags down and leaves them in the hall at the bottom of the stairs. I sit at the kitchen table and wait. I don't even sing any songs in my head when I'm waiting. I don't feel like it.

When the two hands on the clock move so that they are both pointing up at the ceiling there is a noise outside. It sounds like Daddy's car so I start to get off my chair to see if it's him but Uncle Clem points his finger. "Stay there. I'll get it. And remember the deal."

I will remember the deal. He doesn't need to keep saying it. UGH!

He goes out into the hallway and I lean over on my seat to see through the door. He pulls open the door at the front of the house and Daddy walks in. He smiles when he looks down the long hallway and sees me. He walks into the kitchen and bends down with his arms out. I run into them and hold onto his neck. My eyes sting and tears start to come out. Daddy holds me out and looks at me and then up at Uncle Clem.

"Is... everything... okay?"

"Yeah, not a problem, I think little Kiddo here is just tired. Isn't that right, eh?" He nods at me but I look away, into Daddy's shoulder and he keeps talking to him. "Did loads of work for me out in the garden yesterday. And I think someone's little body just isn't used to all the hard work. Ha!"

"Ah, I see. Well it's okay, Kiddo, you can sleep in the car on the way back," Daddy says. He pulls me into his chest and stands up. "We better be off so, Clem. Ange is back at home. Everything is finalised now. As soon as it's out, it's going to a family down in...well not far from here actually. And thanks for looking after this one. Lifesaver."

"Don't mention it, buddy. What else use am I out here in this big place on my own. Any time you need it I'll be glad to have Kiddo back."

"Say goodbye to your uncle, then. And say thank you for letting you stay here." Daddy looks into my face but I close my eyes. "C'mon, don't be rude."

"Never mind, I'm sure we'll be seeing each other again, and you can help me do more work in the garden. That was so helpful." He reaches out and starts to touch my arm but I pull it away. He winks at me "Oh, looks like someone's getting shy again."

Daddy puts me into his car and then goes back into the house to get my bags. I look through the window as him and Uncle Clem are talking. He shakes Daddy's hand then waves at me. When Daddy is walking away to come to the car and he can't see behind him, Uncle Clem puts his finger on his lip like when the teachers at school tell us to "shhhh". I look away and stare at the seat in front of me. I don't want to cry.

Daddy turns on the car and drives away from the big house. I kick the back of his seat. Hard.

"You can go asleep if you're tired Kiddo, it's gonna be ages before we get back home."

I just shake my head.

"No? Aren't you tired?"

I shake my head again.

"Alright, well, do you wanna play *I Spy*?"

Usually I would play *I Spy* and usually I would win, but I don't feel like playing now. I just want everything to be quiet. And I don't want to cry. But I can feel my eyes getting stingy and I can feel tears on my cheeks. I rub them on my hands and look up at the mirror. Daddy should be looking at the road but he is looking at me. He smiles but I don't smile back. I can't. My face won't go into a smile anymore. And I don't want to do deals anymore. Because Uncle Clem did a bad deal and if all the deals are going to be like that then I don't want to do them. I don't want to win at them deals. I only want to win at good deals.

"What's wrong Kiddo?"

I don't say anything and Daddy frowns his face and then looks at the road.

More tears come out of my eyes.

"Daddy..."

"Yeah Kiddo?"

"Y'know the way me and you do deals all the time?"

"Of course, you're the best at deals!"

"Well, I don't wanna do deals anymore."

"What, why not Kiddo?"

"Because, because..." I take a big deep breath and start to

cry really hard. "Because Uncle Clem did a bad deal Daddy."

Daddy goes really slow until the car stops. He takes off his seatbelt and turns around to look at me. He starts to smile, one of his big Daddy smiles, but his face goes all sad when he sees me still crying. I want to stop, but I can't, because I need to tell Daddy. I need to tell him about all the wrong things Uncle Clem did.

I need to tell him about the bad deal.

ABOUT THE AUTHOR

D. T. Moorhouse

D. T. Moorhouse is a secondary school English teacher and self-published author from Ireland. He has a BA in English and Linguistics and an MA in Education from University College Dublin. He splits his time living between Co. Kildare and Dublin, in Ireland.

His first novel, Purple Shadows, was released in July 2020.

Please visit www.dtmoorhousebooks.com for more information.

Empty Colours: Book 2

Yellow Mist

Coming 2021

www.dtmoorhousebooks.com

Contact And Find Out More About D. T. Moorhouse

Email: dtpmoorhouse@gmail.com

Website: http://www.dtmoorhousebooks.com

Facebook: http://www.facebook.com/dtpmoorhouse1

Instagram: http://www.instagram.com/dtmoorhouse

Twitter: http://www.twitter.com/DTMoorhouse1

www.ingramcontent.com/pod-product-compliance
Lightning Source LLC
Chambersburg PA
CBHW031349060726
47590CB00007B/2702